the Boy Who Had (Nearly) Everything

Books for BOYS

IAN WHYBROW
ILLUSTRATED BY TONY ROSS

Children's Books

For my dear chum Dave Mander
and the Minster Buffs

Text copyright © 2000 Ian Whybrow
Illustrations copyright © 2000 Tony Ross

First published in Great Britain in 2000
by Hodder Children's Books
This edition published 2006

A Catalogue record for this book is available
from the British Library.

ISBN-13: 978 0 340 91802 9

Printed in the UK by CPI Bookmarque, Croydon, CR0 4TD

The paper and board used in this paperback by Hodder Children's Books are natural
recyclable products made from wood grown in sustainable forests. The manufacturing
processes conform to the environmental regulations of the country of origin.

Hodder Children's Books
A division of Hachette Children's Books
338 Euston Road, London NW1 3BH
An Hachette Livre UK Company

Meet the O'Mighty Family

Meet the great Rex O'Mighty. Most people call him Triple O'Mighty because he likes things that come in threes. He lives in a mansion that is three times bigger than all the other mansions in the world.

3

And he is three times richer than the next richest man in the world. He got rich because he invented the three most popular snacks of all time . . .

The O'Mighty Triple Megaburger

The O'Mighty Threesy Cheesy Pleasy

The O'Mighty Three-Fishy-Dishy

These are served at the 33,333 O'Mighty Restaurants. Rex tested all

the recipes himself, which is why
his tummy is three times bigger than
anyone else's.

Now meet Mrs Zesty O'Mighty.

She is rich because
when she was a girl,
her father, Zonka
Cola, invented the
most popular cola
on Earth and named
it after her. She
spends half her
time in her gym and
the other half in
clothes shops, looking for the latest
fashions. Her wish is to be the most
elegant woman in the world for
ever.

Zonka Cola thought his daughter was perfect and hoped that one day she would find a perfect husband. His dream came true when she met Triple O'Mighty at a disco and they  won the prize for "Most Interesting Dancers". "They belong together like a Triple Megaburger and Zesty Cola!" sighed Zonka. And he was right.

They got married and *Yum Yum* magazine said . . .

Yes indeed. Now, you know that Triple O'Mighty likes things in threes. That's why he wanted a baby, so there would be three people in his family. This is the famous picture of baby Fries . . .

It was taken when he was three months, three weeks, three days, three hours, and three minutes old. You can see this picture next to the O'Mighty  name in all the restaurants and on all the O'Mighty menu-cards and napkins. Underneath it says . . .

Lucky Fries O'Mighty! This kid has everything!

Oh yes, his busy, busy parents gave him everything except one thing. And he had to wait until his seventh birthday before he found out what it was.

Happy Birthday, Fries!

On that particular day, Fries was
woken by his servant, at noon. The
servant sang "Happy Birthday" and
said, "Hip hip hooray for you, sir.
Look, I have brought you this
special cake."

It was a life-sized model of a dumper truck, covered in special shiny yellow marzipan. The  wheels were made of chocolate, the seat was hard toffee, and the headlights were extra-large lollipops. The steering wheel was made of licorice and the shovel was filled with dolly mixtures, sherbet lemons, candy eggs and fudge.

Fries turned over in bed and yawned. "Take it away!" he ordered. "I had a cake yesterday."

"So you did, sir," said the servant.

"I remember now. I brought you a robot cake that gave you a piggyback round the house. You pushed it out of the upstairs window, didn't you, sir? I'm sorry you didn't like that, sir. Never mind, what would you like me to bring you today?"

"How do I know? You're my servant. You tell me what I'd like!" shouted Fries.

"That will be difficult, since you have everything," said the servant. "But may I suggest, sir, that you have *more* of what you already have?

We could go down to the Fun Room and I could get Gimme-dot-com on your PC for you."

"I'm bored with computer shopping," said Fries. But he had nothing better to do, so he got dressed and went down to the Fun Room.

It was bigger than a barn and full of the chatter of Action Boys and teddies that talked or made rude noises. To reach his PC, Fries had to walk past his collection of miniature cars, all with proper engines, ready to drive. There was a full-size bouncy castle, and a walk-in scale model of Buckingham Palace with all the right furniture.

There was a bow that fired arrows that never missed the target, a solar-powered skateboard, a pair of swimfins that let you break world records every time you went in a swimming pool . . .

"I'm bored with all this junk!" sulked Fries.

"How would you like a nice new theme park, sir?"

"I had a new theme park last week. None of the rides are scary any more. I want my mum and dad. *They'll* think of something I haven't got. Get them for me."

"I'm afraid your father's at his office and Mrs O'Mighty is working out at her gym. They cannot be interrupted," sighed the servant.

Fries threw himself down, banging his heels on the floor, and screamed with rage.

"May I make a small suggestion, sir?" said the servant quickly. "Why don't I look for someone of your own age for you to play with. It might be more fun with someone else joining in."

"What? No way! I'm not sharing!" yelled Fries.

"You don't have to share anything, sir. You could just show a humble person all the things you own and make him jealous. You've never tried that, have you, sir?" said the servant. "It's great fun to have a nice swank and a show-off."

Fries stopped drumming his heels and smiled a spoilt smile.

"I like that idea, servant!" he said. "Very well! Find me somebody humble who I can make jealous. And quickly!"

Meet Billy Humble

In a little cottage in the country, far away from the O'Mighty Mansion lived the Humble family. Mr Humble was a farm worker and drove a tractor. Mrs Humble was a school dinner lady and worked down at the village school.

Billy was their son and he had a funny little dog called Whizz the Fleabag.

They were all sitting round the kitchen table eating sausage, mash and onion gravy, Billy's favourite. And Whizz's favourite, too. Whizz was going bonkers doing all the tricks that Billy had taught him – headstand, spin, roly-poly, speak, somersault, fetch the slipper, die for the Queen, and scratch that flea.

"Can I spoil him, Mum?" said Billy. "Just this once?"

"Oh go on then," smiled Mum.

"He's earned it," said Dad.

"Header!" called Billy and tossed him a nice fat bit of sausage. Quick as a flash, Whizz jumped up and headed it into his dish by the door. Then he did his celebration skid on the tiles, barked "SOSS-A-JISS!" and pounced on his prize.

Just at that moment, there was a mighty roar overhead. All the plates and knives and forks rattled. Three chickens came rushing in through the catflap and Whizz the Fleabag leapt into Billy's lap and stuck his head up Billy's jumper.

Staring open-mouthed, Billy and his mum and dad saw a big black helicopter land in their backyard. The rotors stopped, and out stepped Fries' servant, carrying a large bag. He walked straight into the kitchen without bothering to knock.

He said, "Boy, are you Humble and are you seven years old?"

Mr Humble was humble by name but not by nature. He said, "Not today, thank you," picked up the servant and went to the back door to throw him out into the yard for being so rude.

"Help! Put me down at once!" cried the servant. "I have come to tell you that your son has been chosen to spend the afternoon with the famous Fries O'Mighty, the boy who has everything."

Mr Humble put him down, and said, "You mean as in O'Mighty Restaurants and the O'Mighty Triple Megaburger?"

"Yes. Today it is young Master Fries' birthday," said the servant. "I have been searching for the right sort of boy to enjoy it with him. I found your name – Humble – in the telephone directory. Perfect. If you make Billy come with me, you shall have a very large reward."

It was Mrs Humble who spoke next. "We never take money we haven't earned. And Billy needn't do anything he doesn't want to. What do you say, Billy?"

"I'd like to have a helicopter ride, and so would Whizz," said Billy. "And I'd like to meet the famous boy who has everything. But I must be home in time to muck out my rabbits. Agreed?"

That was agreed and off they went, chop-chop-chop into the sky.

At the Safari Park

Fries was waiting for the helicopter at the train station in his safari park. Down it swooped, making a great wind as it landed. Billy and Whizz got out and Billy held out his hand. He said, "Hello, I'm Billy Humble and this is my dog, Whizz the Fleabag."

Fries said, "I am the famous boy who has everything and I'm not giving you any money."

Billy said, "I was just going to shake hands. Like this . . ." He put out his hand to Whizz. Up went the little dog's right paw.
Shake, shake, shake. "That means we're friends," explained Billy.

"What's friends?" asked Fries.

"Me and Whizz," said Billy. "We look after each other."

So what? Fries thought. His servant looked after him, but *they* weren't friends. He looked at the little dog. He'd never seen anything so cute. But he didn't say so.

Instead, he boasted, "I've got loads of dogs in my kennels. Follow me."

Off they went until they came to a huge building. Inside, there were greyhounds, St Bernards, Dalmatians, poodles – every kind of dog you could think of.

Billy wanted to know their names but Fries said he didn't know. They had keepers to look after them; he never bothered.

"I would, if they were mine," said Billy.

Fries was disappointed that Billy didn't seem jealous yet. "I expect you're dying to have a ride in my safari park train," he swanked.

 "That would be great!" cried Billy. "Will we get to drive? Dad has a tractor and he lets me help drive that sometimes."

"You mean you can drive something? You don't just get driven?" said Fries.

"I love driving. It's excellent fun!" smiled Billy. "Come on. Let's get in the cab and have a go!"

"I'm not sure that that is wise, sir," said the servant. "The driver and fireman are here to serve you."

"Well then, they can teach us what to do," said Billy.

In no time at all, the boys and the little dog were in the cab. They borrowed caps from the driver and fireman and tied a hanky round Whizz's neck. They soon found out which levers to pull. First Billy drove and Fries threw coal on the fire, then they changed places.

Round and round the vast safari

park they puffed, racing the cheetahs, waving to the lions and tigers. Two giraffes crossed necks over the track and made a tunnel for them. Then they stopped to slosh water on the hippos and a crowd of monkeys climbed on board and asked for a ride. What a laugh!

It was such fun, they could have spent the whole afternoon driving the train, but Fries suddenly remembered that he should be gloating and showing off. He pulled on the brake and stopped the train.

The servant, who had been following in the limo ran up with a change of clothes for his young master.

"I bet humble boys wish they had some nice new clean clothes with designer labels, don't they?" gloated Fries.

"Oh, we're not bothered," laughed Billy. "We enjoy getting a bit mucky, don't we Whizz?" As if to answer, Whizz said, "SOSS-A-JISS!"

Then he did
a double
somersault.
Fries was
astonished!
"He can
speak!" he
gasped. "How
does he do that?"

"I trained him to do tricks, but mostly he does things just to please me," said Billy. He tickled Whizz on his favourite spot, under his chin, just behind his ears. Whizz closed his eyes and smiled.

Instead of making Billy jealous, Fries found out what it was like to feel jealous.

"That's what I want for my birthday," he said. "That dog. I want him to do tricks for me. Give him to me. I'll give you anything you want for him," he whined.

"He's not for sale," said Billy sternly.

"You could have my Millennium Dome," said Fries. "It's three times bigger than the one at Greenwich. And you can have my Eye in the Sky. That's three times bigger than the one in London."

"I'm sorry," said Billy firmly. "I'll never let him go."

Fries tried to think quickly. What could he tempt Billy with? There must be something that he'd swap for this little dog.

"Have you ever read what it says on the Triple Megaburger wrapper?" he asked.

"Do you mean about your famous computerized forest that nobody but you has ever been in?" said Billy. "Yes, of course I've read about that. Everybody has."

Fries was pleased with himself.

He was bored with the forest, but he felt sure that Billy would think it was fabulous. All he had to do was offer to swap.

"Servant!" commanded Fries, snapping his fingers. At once, the doors of the limo opened. Seconds later, it was purring along the road, heading for the place that most children would give anything to see.

The Computerized Forest

"Leave us!" commanded Fries when the limousine had dropped them off in the middle of the forest.

"Just press the 'Fetch' button on your mobile when you need me and I'll come and pick you up, sir," said the servant. Then he stepped smartly into the car and sped away.

"Is it always so dark?" said Billy.

"Light!" called Fries, and straight away the whole forest lit up. Fries looked proud. "My dad had this forest programmed to obey my voice," he said. "Spooky!"

At the word "spooky", the forest was washed in a green, misty light. Mechanical owls swooped past their heads – Woo-hoo! – and blinked big yellow eyes.

A pack of wolves
suddenly surrounded
them. They threw
back their heads and
howled.

"Robots!" grinned Fries.

"Cool!" said Billy.
"That's nothing!"
boasted Fries.
"Watch this! Bat
fly-past!" he
called. At once, a
flight of voice-controlled bats

swooped
down in
arrow
formation.

They darted and twisted among the trees, looping the loop when Fries told them to. Then they chased a cloud of flies and swallowed the lot.

"Wicked!" said Billy. "Everybody at school will be so impressed when I tell them about this! It's like magic."

Fries was delighted to see how thrilled Billy was. He called for goblins and trolls. Out from the bushes and up from among the roots of trees swarmed dozens of creatures, some tiny with skin like bark, some huge with extra eyes and heads.

"Let the battle begin!"
commanded Fries.

Explosions! Fireballs! Swords
clashing! Spears flashing! Heads
flying! Billy and Whizz stood and
watched with their mouths open. It
was amazing!

"Freeze!" shouted Fries and the armies vanished.

"That was fantastic!" gasped Billy. "What do you think, Whizz?"

Whizz got all excited. He jumped up. He chased his tail. Finally he did a little salute and did die for the  Queen, just to show how much he was enjoying himself.

Fries thought, "I must have that dog! I just must have him now! He is so cute!" He opened his arms and said to Billy, "You can have all this, plus all the dogs in my kennels.

Plus my safari park. And I'll just have Whizz. OK?"

"No thanks," replied Billy. "But I'd love to have a drink."

Fries took out his gold mobile phone with the diamond keys. "I'll call my servant. He can bring us some Zesty Cola," he said.

"If this was my forest," said Billy, "I'd have little doors on the trees. If you said, 'Drinks!', a door would open and there would be lots of taps inside. And you could turn them on and get any kind of drink you want, strawberry juice, orange fizz, soft ice cream – anything."

"I WANT THAT!" shouted Fries. "It's not fair, you thinking of that. Who told you how to think of that? I only know Zesty Cola!"

"Nobody told me how to think it. I just used my imagination," said Billy.

"I want one of those! Give me an imagination now!" yelled Fries.

Billy didn't know what to say. He had never met anybody as rich or as spoilt as Fries. But now he felt rather sorry for him.

Playing Tarzan

Fries was furious. His servant had told him that he would enjoy playing with another boy. He said it would feel good to make someone jealous. But Fries was feeling jealous – and he didn't like it at all.

Just then, Whizz saw a rope hanging down from a branch. With a whizz and a jump, he caught hold of it with his teeth and started swinging higher and higher.

"He loves that game," laughed Billy. "Shall we have a go?"

"What do we have to do?" said Fries.

"We just swing on some ropes and pretend we're Tarzan."

"Is pretending like using my imagination?" said Fries.

"Exactly!" said Billy. "Just imagine you're a big strong man with a lot of hair on your chest. And imagine this is a jungle."

"And we could save all the animals from a wicked hunter!" shouted Fries.

"There you are! You used your imagination!" smiled Billy.

So Fries pretended to be Tarzan and Billy played the wicked hunter and Whizz played Cheetah the chimp and went "Oo-oo-ooo!" The boys came swinging down from the trees.

Fries
knocked
the invisible
gun out of the
wicked hunter's
hands with a flying
kick. Then he scooped up
Cheetah and swung him to a
safe place on a high branch. Fries
thought it was the best game he had
ever played.

When the limousine came to
fetch them, the servant
found his master
swinging through the
trees with a little
dog tucked
under his arm

shouting, "Ah-ee-ah-ee-ah! Me Tarzan!"

"Be careful, sir!" called the servant. "That is not safe. It is not part of the computer programme invented by the cleverest computer men in the world."

"Who cares about safe?" yelled Fries. "This is fun! And I invented some of this game." Whizz gave him a big wet lick to show how much he enjoyed it too.

Kandy Kingdom

Billy looked at his watch. "Oh no, it's 5.30!" he exclaimed. "Come on, Whizz! We shall have to go, I'm afraid. It's time to muck out my rabbits!"

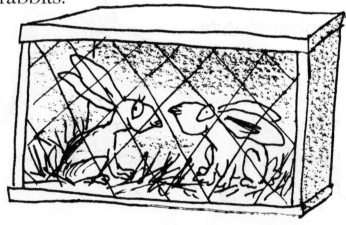

Fries held on tight to the little
dog. He couldn't bear to let him go.

"Get your servants to muck them
out," he said to Billy.

"I haven't got a servant,"
explained Billy. "I'm sure Mum or
Dad would do it for me – but it
wouldn't be the same. The rabbits
would miss their run around with
me. They're only babies. They look
forward to it."

Then Fries had an idea. He swung himself down to the ground. Whizz jumped out of his arms and ran back to Billy.

"Before you go, just come and see my Kandy Kingdom," Fries said. "It's three times bigger than the biggest candy store in the world. You can have any kind of sweets or chocolate you want, any time you want them." Billy was bound to swap his dog for that. No kid could turn down an offer like that.

"Well, I love sweets. And I'd really like to have a quick look before we go back to the helicopter. I'm sure Whizz would, too."

It was Fries' last chance.

The Chocolate Mountain

The limousine raced out of the computerized forest, past the safari park, theme park, the mansion, and the huge dome and wheel, until they reached a glittering three-storey building called Kandy Kingdom.

All the goodies were laid out in alphabetical order. You could start at "A" and have aniseed cough drops or fudge apes or apple flavoured toffee anteaters. Then, you could work your way along the counters and through the shop. At "C", there were great piles of chocolates – chocolates in boxes, chocolate soldiers, chocolate creams, chewy chocs and crunchy chocs.

Whizz did his
sit up and beg
by the chocolate
buttons. Fries
threw one for
him and was
delighted by the
way he caught it on his nose before
he tossed it into his mouth.

"I must have that dog, I must!"
Fries was thinking, his hands
twisting his fingers into knots.

"Do you know what I would do
if I was the owner of the Kandy
Kingdom?" Billy said.

"Aha, but you're not," Fries said
nastily. "And you can't be. Not
unless you give me Whizz to keep!"

"If I was the owner," Billy went on, dreamily, "I would build a chocolate mountain. And I would invite all my friends round to climb it. And we would all have climbing boots and one of those climbing picks. Everyone could chip bits off if they wanted to and eat them."

Billy went on, "And I would
have little caves to explore on the
way up. And all the caves would
have sweets in.
But they would
all be different
and you would
never get sick
of them. And
in one cave,
my friends could
invent any kind of sweet they
liked – like
everlasting
bubble gum, or
dragon sweets, so
you could breathe
out pretend fire.

Or maybe musical sweets that would play your best pop songs when you sucked them. Everybody could share ideas."

Billy had a way of making up things that were a lot more fun than things that you could buy with money. And as for Whizz, scratching away at his ear and looking up at Billy with his little tongue hanging down – how wonderful it would be to have him as a – what was the word for it? Friend?

Suddenly, with a kind of cold, shivery rush, Fries realized that he was going to miss Billy as much as he would miss Whizz.

Having Everything

As they stood outside Kandy
Kingdom waiting for the helicopter,
Fries' gold mobile phone suddenly
burst into song: "Calling Fries,
calling Fries, the luckiest boy in the
world."

"Hello," said Fries.

"Hello, son, this is Dad," said Triple O'Mighty, ringing from his luxurious office. "I have exactly three minutes in my busy day to wish you a happy birthday. Your mother sends you her regards from the gym by the way. She says to ask, have you got everything you want today?"

"No," sniffed Fries. That made the great Triple O'Mighty mighty angry!

"You ungrateful little beast!" he roared. "I have made you three times richer than any boy in the world. I am giving you three minutes of the most valuable time in the world! Your mother gave up three minutes of important jogging time to speak to me about you! What more can you want?"

Poor Fries. With a sob, he dropped his mobile phone on to the ground.

Billy picked it up.

"Hello. Is that Mr O'Mighty? It's Billy Humble here. Do you realize that this is Fries' special day? I don't think you should be shouting at him down the phone. You should be here, making him happy."

"WHATTTT! HOW DARE YOU! WHAT MAKES YOU THINK YOU CAN SPEAK TO ME LIKE THIS?" roared Triple O'Mighty.

"I'm just telling you the truth," said Billy. "Because I'm Fries' friend." He pressed END CALL.

"Your parents won't be getting any money now, you silly boy!" said the servant when he heard what Billy said.

"We don't care about the money," said Billy. "Fries is more important than that."

Fries looked Billy right in the eye and said, "I know what you were doing then. You were looking after me, weren't you? It was like you and Whizz. Do you really mean that?"

Billy looked long and hard at Fries. Finally he said, "What do you think, Whizz?"

Out came the little
dog's right paw.
Shake, shake,
shake.

Billy said, "Well, you're a friend
of Whizz, I can see that. But if you
were a friend of mine, you'd come
home on the bus with me and have
a home-made tea. And you'd help
me muck out the rabbits and feed
them. And maybe you'd take one
home with you and feed it and look
after it yourself. What do you think?"

"I think I'd like to come home

with you, if that's OK . . . and what's a bus?" said Fries O'Mighty. He held out his hand. Billy shook it warmly.

"Come on, I'll show you what a bus is," laughed Billy Humble.

The limousine arrived and the servant jumped out and the helicopter hovered in the sky above their heads, making a terrible noise.

"Sir, can I help you, sir. Do you need a ride anywhere, sir?" shouted the servant.

"Later, perhaps," said Fries. "But at the moment, I shall make my own way with my friends. I have everything I want just now, thank you."